Elizabeth D Cross

An Old Story

And other Poems

Elizabeth D Cross

An Old Story
And other Poems

ISBN/EAN: 9783337397722

Printed in Europe, USA, Canada, Australia, Japan

Cover: Foto ©Andreas Hilbeck / pixelio.de

More available books at **www.hansebooks.com**

An Old Story

AND OTHER POEMS.

BY

ELIZABETH D. CROSS.

SECOND EDITION

LONDON:

LONGMANS, GREEN, AND CO.

1868.

CONTENTS.

I hear the morn,
With her silver horn,
Arousing the valleys fair !
I see the light
On her forehead white,
And the dew on her gleaming hair.

Her rosy hand
On the mountains grand,
Her feet on the sleeping seas,
The islands wake,
On the misty lake,
From their deep and dreamful ease.

B

The darkness dies,
When her shining eyes
Glance over river and bay,
Striking with light
The glaciers white,
And the snow-peaks glimmering grey.

So high, so cold !
Yet she cannot hold
Her calm even there, unshaken,
For many a sound,
Above and around,
The bold bright Day will awaken.

He follows after,
With shouts of laughter !
From his fiery pursuit she flies
O'er valley and hill,
But she hears him still
Break her silence with joyous cries

Aurora.

Her faint heart fails,
And her spirit quails
'Neath the burning glances of Day :
Her fair face fades
In the sunny glades,
Like a dream she dissolves away.

CYNTHIA.

Why was I weary near the happy stars,
 Wandering alone ?—
Why did I find thy Latmos beautiful,
 Endymion ?

And lingering, could not leave the loveliness—
 O heavy night !
When I shed over all his vales and streams
 Mysterious light !

There poppies hung their sleepy crimson heads,
 And berries rare
Hid beneath shining leaves—all gracious forms,
 And creatures fair

I saw, for where my pale rays lit the stream,
    An antlered Deer,
With lustrous gentle eyes, stole down to drink—
    Not without fear !

Thy stately Beech, with wide-spread giant arms,
    Alone stood dark ;
I moved, and every tender leaf was touch'd,
    The ancient bark

Was flecked with shining silver, pure and white.
    And at the roots—
Fairer than any flower of Latmos, or
    The golden fruits

That hang in gardens of the Hesperides—
    Endymion !
I first beheld thee, sleeping thy deep sleep,
    Beloved one !

O I have harmed thee, for my love is death.
    Endymion !
And maketh mad—for even now, alas !
    Unhappy one !

When I but turned upon thee my sad eyes
    (Ah hapless eyes,
So dim with unshed tears) thou did'st grow faint,
    Heaving low sighs ;

And wild disorder'd fancy sudden wrought
    Within thy brain,
Where quiet happy thought, and holy calm
    Erewhile did reign.

O I have harmed thee, for I tempted thee
    To climb so high ;
And I, who love thee as no mortal loves.
    Must see thee die !

I cannot die with thee, Endymion,
    Or, like thee, pass
Away to ease and dreamless rest beneath
    The flowery grass ;

I am immortal, and my deeper woe,
    Unlike to thine,
Thou can'st not fathom, no, nor can'st thou dream
    Of love divine.

Thy pain will cease when thou dost cease to be,
    Endymion !
But mine is limitless, and cannot end.—
    When thou art gone,

Still must I wander through the starry night,
    And Helios,
My brother Helios, (knowing they are mine,
    But my vast loss

Cynthia.

Not knowing,) from fair faces of the flowers
　　Shall kiss my tears,
And marvel why they fell, and how I fare
　　Among the spheres.

AN OLD STORY.

'God above
. . . Creates the love to reward the love.'

So Mark has spoken his mind?
  He always was good and true—
A better man than Michael,
  Who was never the man for you.
And Mark is tall and strong;
  Thank God my child is so blest,
For the strongest are ever the gentlest,
  And the gentlest are always the best!
Alice, my heart was touched,
  And stirred to the very core,
When he told how he loved my darling
  And had loved for years before.

The man's voice trembled and shook,
  When he prayed he might be my son.
And a good light shone in his eyes,
  When he said he had wooed and won.
Alice, my child, it is well,
  And rare to wed the first love—
(For I don't count Michael, my dear,)
  But God has protected my dove.
I don't say Mark's like your father,
  You might search for his like in vain
Through all the wide world, my girl,
  Nor find in the crowds of men
A man of them all who, like him,
  Was of equal heart and brain.
There only was one—and we
  Shall see his like never again.

But your Mark, I love him well,
  He is good, and strong, and true.

An Old Story.

And he seems to bring back the days
    When I was a girl like you ;
Like you, but not so gentle,
    For you have a touch and a trace
Of your father, and I was wilful,
    Wayward, and wild; but my face,
Though so altered now, was like yours,
    My daughter, the face, and the hair;
" My glory" my mother called it,
    For the brightness and length were rare.
And it seems like yesterday, Alice,
    Only like yesterday,
When the long dark locks were shorn,
    My glory was taken away.
How strange it seems to me now,
    That I thought, as I watched it fall,
God takes that too—I believed
    He was wroth, and had taken all.
For I lay in a terrible fever,
    And my heart was turned to stone;

They hardly knew me, I was so changed,
  When the cruel fever was gone.
My mother wept to see me,
  But I shed never a tear,
My heart within was hard as stone,
  And knew neither hope nor fear.
For I loved (not your father Alice),
  Loved, and had been deceived,
It would have saved a world of woe
  Never to have believed ;—
So I thought then, not now;
  But your father always said, "Nay,
Better believe and suffer,
  Than never to trust," he would say.
And in after years, my girl,
  When I set the gained by the lost,
I'd have borne it all, and ten times more,
  Nor ever have counted the cost.
How little we know !—when I thought that I,
  Like a helmless ship, was cast

On the hard bleak rocks of some desert coast,
　God was guiding me, sure and fast,
Leading me home by wonderful ways,
　To a blessed haven at last.

For in those days I used to sit
　Spinning, outside in the air,
I was too weak yet to work in the house,
　Or walk to the village fair.
And as I sat spinning as if for life,
　Too stunned to think, or to feel,
('The sun, I remember, was low in the west,)
　A shadow darkened the wheel—
I did not stop, for I thought it would move.
　To pass our way there were few,
But the shadow remained, and I turned at last,
　And there was my cousin Hugh.
And he was bending a look on me
　That I shall never forget,

It is more than thirty years since then,
  But well I can see it yet.
I knew not what was the thought in his heart,
  But his face was transfigured, and shone,
And his great blue eyes were filled with tears,—
  But even while I looked he was gone.

My spinning was done when the sun was set,
  And when I entered the door,
I said that I thought my cousin Hugh
  Might have passed an hour before.
My mother turned away from me,
  She answered sharp, and fast,
" Well, it's not the first time he's passed this way,
  And maybe it isn't the last."
And then her voice grew softer, and changed,
  And she said, " Was he ever away,
When you were down with the fever, child—
  Did he leave us night or day ?

Who ran to the town so quickly,
 And brought the wise docter to save ?
If it had not been for your cousin Hugh
 You might have been in your grave !"
Then I wished I was not so wicked,
 Had a heart of flesh, not of stone,
I wished I could weep like all good folks,
 And was not quite changed, and alone.
And so the next time the shadow passed,
 And the footstep that I knew,
I thought I would speak,—but I found not a word
 To say to my cousin Hugh.
At last he came and did not pass,
 But sat on the bench by the door,
And tried to talk, as we used to talk
 In the happy days of yore, .
(When I was a child, and he was a child,
 And would help me when I fell,
And though he bore a burden himself,
 Would carry my basket as well.)

And many a time and hard I strove
   The thanks in my heart to say,
I only heard the sound of the wheel,
   My words seemed to die away.
But when he asked, in a doubtful voice,
   If it was not too much to pray
That he might have a lock of the hair
   Was so cruelly shorn one day,
I was glad to think there was anything
   He fancied, that I could give,
For I was so poor in thanks, and in all
   That makes it worth while to live.
So I quickly rose to find him a lock,
   For my mother kept the hair
In the old oak chest in the inner room,
   And while I was searching there,
My mother came in, looking glad, and I said,
   "May I give some to cousin Hugh?"
She answered, " I'd give whatever he asks
   To your cousin, if I were you."

I did not see the sense of her words—
  I understood little—then,
But I took a long long curling lock,
  And went out to Hugh again.
His eyes were fixed on the setting sun,
  His face was pale and kind,
Courteous and gentle the thanks he gave,
  As well I can bring to mind
But when he had the hair in his hand,
  He seemed to forget I was there,
And fell to saying such sweet strange things.
  And all to a lock of hair !
I could not follow the words he said—
  Sometimes they seemed quite wild,
And then I saw him kiss the hair,
  And then he sobbed like a child.
And while I was wondering more and more.
  And thought it could hardly be true,
That any man should be weeping thus—
  And such a strong man as Hugh—

I seemed to wake from a woful dream,
 My spinning began to shake,
And my heart was a heart of flesh, that swelled,
 And throbbed as though it would break.
Then the long-gathering storm of tears
 Fell fast, but not for grief,
As you have seen the heavy rain
 Bring the sad air relief.
And I could see all things clearly now,
 And by the wonderful grace
Of God, could know and could understand,
 Not darkly, but face to face.
Not even to you, my daughter,
 All that passed that night can I tell,
Nor all the words that were spoken,
 Though I remember them well.
But before the end of the evening
 I was as happy as you,
I had wealth untold who was once so poor,
 And my troth was plighted to Hugh.

But I don't think I ever thanked him
  For saving my life and me,
Unless the love of my whole life long
  Some little thanks might be.
For, Alice, the false love fades,—
  Falls from the heart like a garment old,
Dies like the dew in the light of the sun,
  Is forgot as a tale that is told.
But the power no gold can give,
  That over all prevails,
Is the love that lives through sorrow,
  The faith that never fails ;
That many waters cannot quench,
  Nor whispering tongues can chill,
Nor doubt, nor any fear come near,
  Absence, nor death can kill.
And with this power your father wooed,
  And with this wealth he won.
Mark, too, is a man knows how to win—
  He is to be my son.

Then, Alice, my daughter, thank God
For the gift of a good man's love :
It is the best of all blessings
That come to us from above.'

LYCORIS.

Beautiful Lycoris, lying
  Underneath the Ilex tree,
Lightly laughing, softly sighing,
  Lifted languid eyes on me.
Beautiful Lycoris, lying
  Underneath the Ilex tree,
Told me half in jest, half sighing.
  How sweet Doris died for me :
Died, when chestnut leaves were dying,
  Falling fast in crimson showers,
All the purple grapes were gathered.
  And among the fading flowers
Cold winds crept. and birds were flying
  Home, across the wintry sea,
Then sweet Doris died for me.

Lightly laughing, gently sighing,
   Softly glancing spake to me
Beautiful Lycoris, lying
   Underneath the Ilex tree.

And I listened, breathless, leaning
   Hard against the Ilex tree,
Listened (seeing all the meaning
   Of her dark eyes' treachery)
To the tale so lightly told.
   Then darkness, swift and thick, closed o'er me,
And I heard no more.—
   But in vision came before me,
Pale, with tresses of pure gold,
   Not Lycoris, but a maiden,
Singing, as she sang of yore,
   Ere I went beyond the sea,—
Fled, believing false and traitrous
   Words Lycoris spake to me :—

Lycoris.

Came, with tender eyes love-laden,
    Shining with the light of truth,
Not Lycoris, but a maiden
    In the glory of her youth.
But she passed me, singing, singing,
    Through the forest passed away,
And I woke to agony,
    In Lycoris' arms I lay.
In mine ears the sweet song ringing,
    In my heart the tender grace
Of the happy eyes love-laden,
    And the fair young face
Of the guileless gentle maiden,
    Who was dead for me.
Woke, to see the treachery
    Of the dark eyes bent above me,
    And the loose locks floating free.
From those eyes fell glittering tears,
    (Lightly could she laugh and weep),

And she murmured hopes and fears.—
Then I cursed her, low and deep,
And her black locks, loosely flying,
And her dark eyes' treachery,—
Beautiful Lycoris, lying
Underneath the Ilex tree.

NATHALIE.

In Alsace, pleasant Alsace,
  In the broad land of France,
There grew an ancient garden,
  A garden and pleasaunce.

The sweet Provençal roses
  In many a parterre blew,
The red, and white, and damask,
  Roses, and lilies too.

Among the linden blossoms
  Went murmuring the bee ;
The soft air stirred the branches,
  And birds made melody.

It was long ago, in Alsace,
   In the old time golden-fair,
When hearts were true—in Alsace,
   When love and faith were there.

Under the lindens an old man
   Sat dreaming in the sun,
Upon his gracious lips a smile,
   As though his work were done.

His grey head and his sightless eyes
   Were lifted, as in praise
For the sweet sounds he still might hear,
   In the long summer days.

Beside him played his grandchild,
   As fair a little maid,
As ever on the banks of Rhine,
   In hanging garden strayed;

Her laugh was sweeter in his ear
    Than song of any bird ;
Her voice was like a lost voice,
    Might never more be heard.

' Grandfather,' said the little maid,
    ' Why do you talk and smile,
As though with pleasant company
    The time you did beguile ?

' You sit alone, grandfather,
    And yet you look so gay,
That to be old and blind like you,
    I have wished many a day ! '

' Nay, never wish that thou wert blind,
    My little Nathalie,
Pray to have won, if thou art old,
    So sweet a memory ;

‘ For I am never quite alone :
 Fond fancies fill my mind,
And a dear face that bends o’er me
 I see, though I am blind.

‘ Often to comfort me she comes,
 And her least word to me
Is of more worth than all the wit
 Of the best company.

‘ What thou dost say, my little maid,
 To-day, I may forget ;
What she said fifty years ago,
 I can remember yet.’

‘ But, grandfather, who is she
 That I have never seen ?
She must be a magician, or
 Perhaps the Fairy Queen.’

' Dearer she is, more pitiful,
   Than any Fairy Queen,
And she is always beautiful,
   And always is eighteen ! '

' Grandfather, that *is* magic,
   For fifty years ago,
You said, yet she is still eighteen :
   Now how can that be so ? '

' Listen, and thou shalt understand,
   My little Nathalie,
How she must always be eighteen,
   And beautiful for me.

' Long, long ago, my darling,
   Within these garden walls,
Where now for thee the roses blow,
   For thee the linnet calls,

' There grew another Nathalie,
  With just thine eyes and hair,
Thy voice, too, is like hers ; but thou
  Wilt never be so fair.

' This Nathalie was greatly loved
  By one, who could not tell,
'(So coy and maidenly she was)
  If she too loved him well.

' Therefore the youth was often sad,
  But sometimes full of bliss,
When he might linger long with her.
  On such a day as this.

' Ah ! he was then so happy
  That he almost forgot
A pain that pressed upon his eyes.
  And day or night ceased not.

· And when the pain grew heavier,
    To a far city, then,
His lady bade him go, to seek
    The counsel of wise men.

' The great physician shook his head,
    Nor cure, nor hope could find ;—
" Nothing can now avert thy doom,
    One month, and thou art blind."

' The youth fell down in heavy swoon,
    For love and light, to him,
Were lost he thought for evermore,
    And the dread phantom dim,

' That we call death, was to this man
    As welcome as a friend,
But unto them who call for it
    How rarely comes the end !

' Out of the swoon where he was blest
　　He woke to anguish sore,
For his first thought was that his love
　　He now must see no more.

' He had no tender mother
　　To make his sorrow less,
No father, and no brother,
　　No sister to caress.

' In the far city he would stay,
　　And there, when light was gone,
Alone, in darkness and despair,
　　His life should linger on.

' To his lost love at last he wrote.
　　The letter ran : Sweetheart,
There is no hope, my fate is sealed,
　　And thou and I must part.

' But do not let thy dear heart grieve
  For me, whose joy is flown ;
Live thou thy life, that is, to me,
  Far dearer than my own.

' I stay in the great city, where
  Is much to hear and learn,
And doubt not thou, that I, in time,
  Content and peace may earn.

' Often shall tidings come to me
  Of thee and thy sweet life,
And how, one day, a happier man
  Has won thee for his wife.

' And do not dream that I regret
  The love that cannot die,
That love shall lighten my dark days,—
  My life is memory.

' Farewell, thou dearest woman,
  The way thou leddest me
I follow, till I reach the land
  Where all the blind shall see.

' Then through the noisy city streets
  He wandered wearily ;
In all that crowd there was not one
  More sad and lone than he.

' But after many days were passed,
  And he least looked for joy,
Just as the sun set, to his door
  There rode a fair-haired boy.

' He knew his lady's little page,
  His heart beat loud and fast,
While swifter than a shadow glides,
  Down to the gate he passed.

' The boy was weary, travel-stained,
　And well his vow had kept,
For since his lady's letter left
　Her hand he had not slept.

' A little letter—Dost thou wish
　To break my heart ? it said,
Come home, come home, if thou delay.
　Dear, thou wilt find me dead !

' False lover, and unfaithful,
　To leave me here to weep,
My mother cannot comfort me,
　My father cannot keep

' His kind eyes from o'erflowing,
　When he looks upon my woe !
Come, for I love thee, though unkind
　And cold I seemed, I know.

'Come, for I dare no longer weep ;
　　Dost thou not know, my dear,
These eyes must serve both thee and me
　　For many a happy year ?

'Come, for we have so little time,
　　Our wedding day draws nigh,—
My mind is changeful, thou wilt say
　　As is an April sky !

'I am a woman (reason fair),
　　And though I said thee nay
So often, yet I now would fain
　　Hurry our wedding day !

'Farewell, dear heart, no happier man
　　Shall win me for his wife,
Thou art far dearer than before,
　　My only love and life !　.　.　.

'Now is my story longer grown,
  My little Nathalie,
Than thou dost care to hear, or I
  Had meant to tell to thee.

'When last I looked upon her face,
  The fairest ever seen,
She wore her bridal robes and wreath,
  And she was just eighteen.

'She was thy mother's mother, child,—
  Sometimes, they say, a trace
Thou bearest, in thy looks and ways,
  Of her surpassing grace.

'Too soon, too soon she left me,
  That other Nathalie,—
My moon, my star, the only light
  Of the dark world for me.'   .

' Grandfather,' said the little maid,
' Teach me, I pray, to be
Like her, who was so kind and true—
That other Nathalie.'

THE WILD ROSES.

'Dans la vie, garde-toi de rien différer.'

I walked in the joyous morning,
    The morning of June and life,
Ere the birds had ceased to warble
    Their sweetest of love and strife ;

I walked alone, in the morning,
    And who so glad as I
When I saw the pale wild roses
    Hang from the branch on high !

Fairer than stars were the roses,
    Faint was the fragrance and rare,
Not any flower in the garden
    Could with those roses compare.

The Wild Roses.

But the day was all before me,
  The tumult of youth's delight,
Why bear a burden of roses
  Before the calm of the night ?

Let them stay awhile to gladden
  The air, and the earth below,
With tender beauty and sweetness
  They cannot choose but bestow.

So I kissed the roses, and lightly
  I breathed of their breath divine ;
It is time when I come back, I said,
  To make the sweet roses mine.

I went in the gladsome morning,
  I said, we part for an hour,
The branch of wild roses trembled,
  The dew was on every flower.

I returned in the joyless evening,
　I yearned with passion then,
For the pale and peerless roses,
　I never should see again.

For another had taken delight
　In colour and perfume rare,
And another hand had gathered
　My roses beyond compare.

From east to west I may wander,
　Wherever the sun doth shine,
I never shall find the wild roses,
　The roses I thought were mine.

SCHÖNFELS.

'Ah! I envy thee those trees, brother Merlin, and their fresh waving, for here, in Paris, no green leaves rustle; and early and late, I hear nothing but the rattle of carriages, hammering, scolding, and the jingle of the piano.'

I listen to the ceaseless tide
    That roars in Paris, day and night;
I listen, but my heart is far
    In the dear land of my delight.

I tread again the paths we trod,
    Gaze on the scenes we found so fair;
Cold cruel winter may come here,
    But surely it is summer there!

And do you sometimes bring to mind
  The mountain air, the flowers that grew ?
The scarlet berries bright as flame,
  The moss and fern, the gentians blue,

The silence of the woodland way,
  Darkness, and mystery of green ;
The whispered prophecy of pines,
  The shafts of light let down between,

That fell fantastic on the moss,
  Betraying many a treasure there ;
Made yellow lichen glow like gold,
  And lighted eyes, and lips, and hair ;

Like laughter smote the slender stream,
  And into amber turned the grey,
Though murmuring plaintive in the shade,
  Then every sad note changed to gay.

And how we waited, till the west
   Was troubled with the coming pain
Of parting—and the Jungfrau flushed
   With her old memories again !

In violet Pilatus robed,
   An hour of triumph this for him ;
How close the three weird sisters crouched,
   To mutter in the twilight dim !

Can you remember how the lake
   Was sometimes sapphire, sometimes pale ?
At morn reflecting every cloud,
   At eve the careless passing sail

Was bathed in glory, gliding through
   A pathway broad of burnished gold,
Flung down from heaven across the blue,
   Splendid as the dream-stair of old.

Lucerne was envious, darkly gloomed
  Her distant waters ; hard as steel,
And cold and passive as despair
  She lay, as she should never feel

Warm sunlight on her bosom more ;
  As though she hardly hoped the moon
Would rise behind the hill, and change
  Dark waters into silver soon.

Have you forgot how passion-pale
  She rose that night ? how fair and wan,
Hanging so low, as she would fain
  Stoop down to wake Endymion ?

Perhaps you smile, with winter here,
  That one should dream of summer yet ;
But though December preaches well,
  He cannot teach me to forget.

I shudder in the angry blast,
  To think the snow is softly laid,
Like cerements on a fair dead face,
  O'er hills and valleys where we strayed.

To think the music of the stream
  Is silent now, perplexes me,—
That birds that sang so sweet are flown,
  And bare and cold are bower and tree,

Beneath whose shades we lingered long.
  They will return,—the leaves and flowers,
The birds will all come back again,
  But not the wonder-working powers

Of spring herself, or summer suns,
  Or gracious autumn can restore
The charm, the glory once was theirs,
  That which has been, but is no more.

And other eyes may watch the light
   Of sunset on the champaign vast,
Others may wander in the woods,
   All our possessions in the past—

The past that pales and fades away,
   That only I remember yet,
Sometimes I hope that you recall,
   And sometimes trust that you forget.

LOVE AND PITY.

'Pity is akin to love.'

Love sought his sister Pity, (whom he scorned
　　An hour ago,)
Tears in his bright eyes, in his trembling hands
　　A flaccid bow

And broken arrows—pale his rosy lips,
　　And he made moan,
While Pity wandered in the flowery fields
　　Of Paradise, alone.

But when she heard Love's dear voice, quick she
　　　turned
　　Her eyes divine,
And when she saw him fallen amid the flowers,
　　She cried, 'O Eros mine!'

And 'Eros, Eros' echoed through the woods,
    While Pity pressed
The darling boy upon her gentle heart.
    And tenderly caressed ;

Much marvelling that his cheek was pale, and
    quenched
    The lustre of his eye,
'O Love, what ails thee, wherefore weepest thou ?'
    Love moaned, 'I die !'

'O my sweet sister, see my arrows broke
    Against the stone
Of hearts that know not thee—behold I die,
    My power is gone !'

But Pity kissed him, and the light of life
    Rekindled in his eye,
The fading rose returned to lip and cheek ;
    Love cannot die

E

When he and Pity in the happy fields
Together rove ;
But he who knows not Pity, cannot know
Her brother, Love !

In the great primeval forest,
  Long ago, I stood
To breathe the free air they had breathed,
  The wild men of my blood.

To see their happy hunting-grounds,
  While back my memory ran
To deeds of thine, heroic maid,
  Daughter of Pohetan !

The dark pines bowed and whispered,
  ' Why dost thou longer roam
· A stranger in the other lands
  ' When here is thy true home ?

' Here, where thy fathers hunted
  ' The wild deer and the boar,
' Where dark-eyed maidens of thy race
  ' Loved well, in days of yore.'

Ah, friendly pines ! another tale
  That day was told to me ;
How shall I trust your murmurings
  That sound so tenderly !

Your treacherous graces tempted,
  Your subtle charms beguiled
The darling from his mother's breast,
  The father's favourite child !

I met a mournful woman there,
  Who wandered in the wood ;
And while I marvelled what might cause
  So sorrowful a mood,

A Virginian's Tale.

The child that walked beside her
  Looked up, with soft blue eyes,
And to my questions of the way
  Returned me sweet replies.

Then, with a woman's courtesy,
  She offered humble cheer,
And showed me that the low log house,
  Her mother's home, was near.

But as we went, the mother's eyes
  Turned, with such wistful pain,
To the dark pines, as they would win
  Some lost one back again.

'Mother will always fancy, Sir,'
  The little maiden said,
'That still my brother wanders there,—
  She cannot think him dead.'

· Where did he go ?' I asked ;—then her
    Sad tale the mother told.
· He was my youngest and my best,
    And only five years old.

' He was the fairest of the flock—
    The neighbours say the same—
But we have lost him, and I think
    That we were all to blame.

· I let him follow father, to
    The forest here one day,
And then the child grew weary,
    And would no longer stay.

· His father felled the forest trees,
    The boy would often roam
As far with him—often alone—
    And safely he came home.

' But how he missed his way that day
    God knows—I cannot tell :
His home was near—the forest paths
    And tracks he knew so well.

' I thought all day that he had stayed
    With father and his men,
But when without him they returned,
    Ah ! in what terror then

' We wandered through these woods all night.
    Seeking our little son,
Seeking him far, but found him not
    When the long night was done :

' Then the whole village went to search,
    For they all loved the boy :
To every man and woman there
    To find him had been joy.

‘ They sought him high, they sought him low,
 With many a shout and cry ;
They only heard the bobolink
 And mocking-bird reply.

‘ They only saw the squirrels play,
 And leap from tree to tree,
The squirrels and young foxes there,
 That sported merrily.

‘ But of my child, for many days,
 They nothing saw or heard.
At last, deep in the wood, like nests
 Forsaken by the bird,

‘ They came on houses he had built—
 Small huts of twig and leaf,
Wherewith awhile he had beguiled
 His loneliness and grief.

A Virginian's Tale.

' And all so neatly made ! such ways
　　He had, and pretty wit,—
And then we found his little shoes,
　　And socks that I had knit.

' And once, far off, on the rough trunk
　　Of a great fallen tree,
Some hunters found his yellow hair—
　　This lock they brought to me.

' They say that he is dead; but, Sir,
　　At night I often hear
The child call, " Father, father,"
　　His voice is small and clear.

' But when I rise to search for him
　　Then he is always gone,
And though the sweet voice sounded near,
　　Too far he wanders on.'　.　.　.

Ah ! who can comfort now, I mused,
   This mother so forlorn,
Whose cheek is wasted with her woe,
   Her eyes with searching worn ?

But to the living child I turned,
   So sweet and fair a maid,
And thought that in such sunshine
   Her grief must surely fade.

The great primeval forest, then,
   For many days I crossed,
Nor did I dream of Indian queens,
   But only of the lost.

At night, beside my camp fire, heard
   The sound of little feet,
And ' Father, father,' calling,
   A voice forlorn and sweet.

A RIVER.

'Dieu Créateur pardonne à leur démence ;
  Ils s'étaient faits les échos de leurs sons,
Ne sachant pas qu'en une chaîne immense,
  Non pour nous seuls, mais pour tous nous naissons.'

——Tell you another story ?
  But the evening is almost gone,——
Yet shall it be sad or gay,
  This story of many a one ?

Nay, how wise you have grown to-night !
  Wise, with the wisdom of few——
' Let it either be grave or glad,
  If only it may be true !'

Well, I remember a story,
　It hardly was meant for you,
Or gay, or sad, I know not,
　But I know that it may be true.

The story is all of a river
　Flowing so full and deep,
But the bed of the river was narrow
　And the rocky sides were steep.

It was born far away in the mountains,
　High up in the happy hills ;
It came leaping and dancing downward,
　Fed by a hundred rills,

Till it grew a wealth of water,
　Flowing so swift and strong
That nothing could follow after,
　Or hinder its flowing long.

It heeded never the gardens,
   Where the flowers lay drooping and wan,
Nor stayed by the thirsty meadows,
   Where the sun so fiercely shone.

A wilful, headlong river,
   That turned not to left or right,
You might hear the passionate rushing
   Far in the silent night.

' Where was it hasting, the river,
   Flowing so straight and true ? '
I cannot tell you, my darling,
   For only the river knew.

Nay, do not smile, to the river
   It was matter of life and death ;
To have watched it hurrying onward
   Had taken away your breath.

Perchance in depths of a far blue lake
   Its waters yearned to rest ;
Perchance the many-voiced sea had called
   The river home to his breast.

Whatever the dream, it might not be ;
   For they laid great stones, and hard,
In the bed of the shining river,
   And all its purpose marred.

And if you had heard the sobbing
   Of waters, the passionate moan,
You would have thought a human heart
   Was breaking against the stone.

Yet now, in the thirsty meadows
   Is water enough and to spare,—
The drooping flowers in the gardens
   Raise faces so fresh and fair !

Well—was it well for the river?
   You think, ' it was better far,'—
I cannot tell : is the trailing light
   _ Sweet to the falling star ?

But if you had heard the sobbing
   Of waters, the passionate moan,
You would have thought a human heart
   Was breaking against the stone.

Good night, good night, my darling.
   The day is ended and gone,
So now I think it is time to sleep,
   For all my stories are done.

THE FALCON.

I.

THE FLIGHT OF THE FALCON.

‘ How the light light love, he has wings to fly.’

Lilias and Christabel
Have each a bird that they love well.

Dove and love-bird that they prize ;
I had a falcon, with wild eyes.

That her turtle flieth not,
Sweet Christabel hath built a cot ;

A golden cage, a prison rare,
Lilias hath wrought with care.

Jesses nor hood my falcon knew,
And where he listed there he flew ;

But ever, were it east or west,
His falconry was on my breast.

My father gave high towers three,
To Lilias, Christabel, and me ;

In the space between the towers,
He set for us the fairest flowers ;—

For them, white rose and eglantine,—
The myrtle and red rose were mine.

And in our castle by the sea
Morn and eve were sweet to me.

Till one day Lilias did espy
(Gazing from her lattice high)

F

A glittering company appear,
The sunlight flashed on crest and spear ;

I leaned to look on knights so gay,
And my proud falcon flew away.

In wrath he flew beyond the sea,
Nor ever hath come back to me.

I spake no word, I shed no tear,
Lilias and Christabel were near,

Who straight began to make sweet moan,
And blame me that my bird was flown.

Peace, peace, I pray, dear Christabel,
And Lilias that I love so well,

If my wild falcon would away,
Think ye that I would bid him stay ?

Sigh not, ladies, neither sorrow,
To every night there comes a morrow,

And it may be, o'er land or sea,
My falcon will come back to me.

II.

LAMENT FOR THE FALCON.

'And're gehen mir vorüber
Und ich schaue sie nicht an.'

Come back, my bird, come back to me !
  For weary is the lingering day,
Nor heaven is blue, nor earth is bright.
  Since my wild falcon flew away.

When morning breaks, I long for night.
  And when the night comes, woe is me !
For dreaming that my bird is dead,—
  Come back again, come back to me !

For sweet things change, and fade, and die,
　None will remain of all we see,
While yet our little moment lives,
　Come back, my bird, come back to me !

And many faces come and go,
　Light words are spoken, jests are free,
For lips may smile, when hearts are stone,
　Come back, my bird, come back to me !

O wilt thou never come again ?
　Long, long, I look across the sea,
While laughter floats in bower and hall,
　I weep, my bird, I weep for thee.

Fly o'er the weary winter sea,
　O, my wild bird, fly home to me !
Across the seas, beyond the stars,
　My falcon, I will follow thee !

III.

THE RETURN OF THE FALCON.

' Trop menu le fil casse.'

Lilias and Christabel,
Sweet ladies that I love so well.

Take off, take off the gown of grey,
Spindle and distaff put away,

Of ermine fair, and cramoisy,
Busk ye in all the bravery,

And let your silver laughter ring,
More sweet than any song ye sing.

But as for me, mine eyes are dim,
O'er every sense a mist doth swim,

The Falcon.

For o'er strange lands beyond the sea
My falcon has come back to me !

Kiss me, ladies, clasp me well,
Dear Lilias and Christabel,

For this I know, that joy's excess
Is near akin to bitterness ;

And though I lived in spite of sorrow,
I think that I shall die to-morrow,

So weary is my spirit grown,
With watching for my falcon flown,

So tired my heart of sad endeavour,
To call to him who heard me never.

Too far beyond the dreary sea,
My falcon flew away from me.

And now I only long for rest,
Although my bird is on my breast,

And though his wild eyes bend on me
The light of lights I longed to see.

'Tis not the blessing is too great,
But this—the blessing comes too late—

And the life I fain would borrow
For my love, was spent on sorrow.

And now remains but the long sleep
When I shall neither watch nor weep,

But wake to find that love is rest,
In island-valleys of the blest.

'CARI LUOGHI.'

So often I walk with you
   Through the streets of the little town !
Do you remember the quaint
   Queer way they went up and down ?

Do you remember the gables,
   The wonderful arched gateway,
The carved old doors with the Latin
   Inscriptions, and colours so gay ?

How the mountains looked down on the townlet.
   The blue lake reflected the spire
Of the church, set away on the hillside,
   From danger of flood, or of fire ?

(For the lake, though it lay so placid,
　So fair, at our feet, and still,
Could rage and storm in the winter,
　And all the wide valley would fill.)

How the statues of saints bent to bless us !
　The lovely Madonna and Child
Looked down from their high and dark places
　Tenderly on us, and smiled.

I leaned on your arm, I remember,
　We thought the days ended too soon—
We did not then dream that December
　Could follow so closely on June.

THE CHARIOTEER.

' A good man in his dark strivings may still be conscious of the right
way.'

A regal chariot on golden wheels,
  Full stored with princely gear,
Two noble steeds that seem of equal fire,
  To the proud Charioteer.

With eager step, bright hair, and smiling lip,
  He leaps into the car,
His eyes are true, as those of highest souls,
  And gentle as theirs are.

An angel whispers, as he grasps the reins,
  ' Of these twin-steeds of thine,
One is all evil, and hath low desires,
  One only is divine.'

With careless hand he guides, and hopeful heart,
  His eyes are on the height,
Where morning sunshine strikes the sparkling
    snow,
  Crowning the crag with light.

The rolling hours bring heavy heat of noon,
  The creeping mist descends,
The mountain tops and the blue heav'ns are hid,
  And the clear pathway ends.

He strains his aching eyes, the horses plunge,
  In maddening terror rear,
One drags him down, one struggles upward still,
  Though blinded with his fear.

'Obey the higher creature, curb the base'—
    The angel whispers low,
But the high path is shrouded from his sight,
    The valley smiles below.

      *   *   *   *   *

Steep was the upward way, but this is death,
    Darkness, and fell despair,
O for the light of morning on the heights,
    And the keen mountain air !

'The pathway does not end, though it be hid
    A moment by the mist,
Have faith—but little time remains—the day
    Is over ere thou wist,'

The angel says ; and he obeys, though long
    Seems now the weary way,
Bright hope flies not beside him, as of yore,
    Cold grows the dying day.

Yet calm upon his troubled spirit falls,
  The journey's end is near,
And once again he hears the angel's voice,
  ' The gates of heaven appear ! '

Then did he mourn—' Ah, lord, but not for me.
  How can I enter now,
So travel-stained, with fainting steeds, and marks
  Of anguish on my brow ? '

The angel answered, ' In thy Father's court,
  These grey hairs, and quenched fires,
Are dearer than the joyous pride of youth,
  High hopes, and wide desires.'

MAY.

'Sentiers où l'herbe se balance,
O vallons, coteaux, bois chevelus,
Pourquoi ce deuil et ce silence?
—Celui qui venait ne vient plus.'

O come ! for it passeth so quickly,
Like all that is good and fair,
Come, while the subtle sweetness
Lingereth still in the air.

The chestnut is laden with stately flowers,
The thorn is in bridal white,
The odorous lilac is heavy with bloom,
And yieldeth a rare delight !

Laburnums are drooping with gold for you,
  And lilies are pale with love,
Thinking to die ere they see you again,
  They weep when the stars are above.

The cedar is weary of waiting,
  And watching the shadows pass,
Blown by the west wind so lightly,
  Over the long waving grass.

When I smiled to the blossoming sycamore,
  The sycamore only sighed,
Then trembled—with such a heavy sigh.
  To the sycamore's I replied.

O come ! in this passionate springtime
  Is less of joy than of pain,
The glory and loveliness ours to-day
  May never be ours again.

Come, dear, for my heart is so heavy,
　　O come ! and it will rejoice,
It is but to look in your eyes, my friend,
　　It is but to hear your voice !

OTILLIA.

' Ich habe gelebt und geliebet.

I often would, my Otillie,
  We might grow old together,
And I your raven locks might see
  Blanch in life's winter weather :

For then I swear each silver hair
  Would dearer grow to me,
Thy fading form with what fond care
  I'd cherish Otillie !

But that small voice, so still and cold,
  Whispers it may not be ;
Tells me I never shall grow old
  With thee, my Otillie !

G

Otillia.

Changeless for me is my desire
    The crimson flower thy mouth,
Those lustrous eyes that glow with fire
    And sunshine of the South.

The perfect curves of cheek and chin,
    Unclouded brow, sweet breath.
O my delight ! that I might win
    More days from jealous Death :

That for a little while might cease
    The quick relentless flight
Of hurrying hours, that bring release
    For thee—for me, the night.

When a new lover's arms are thrown
    Around thee, Otillie,
Remember I loved thee alone,—
    Ah, dear ! remember me.

And yet if he should worthy prove
  Of my fair world—thy heart—
Then fear not to forget me, love,
  But give—give all thou art!

For I would have thee wholly blest—
  And highest life can be
Only in giving all exprest.
  My darling Otillie!

Love, therefore, ere thou reach that heaven
  Where I wait thee, my wife,
Thank God that even here is given
  To me a perfect life.

SONG.

I shall meet my love to-morrow.
  My love is fair and kind,
And she can banish sorrow
  Back to time out of mind.

Whither she goes I follow,
  Knowing so well the way—
Straighter than flight of swallow—
  Will lead to heaven one day.

I shall meet my love to-morrow—
  Ah! would that many a one
Could quite forget his sorrow,
  Could love as I have done !

AUGUST IN ENGLAND.

'La mort dans l'âme.'

Tall spears of flowering grass, the heather's bloom.
    Red apples on the bough,
A yellow leaf on the fair fluttering birch,
    And the thick bracken now.

Bright gaudy poppies, and pale chicory,
    Wild thyme, and blue corn-flower,
The trailing grace of white convolvulus,
    And yellow crowfoot's dower.

The golden sunlight upon mellowing corn.
    Sweet clover in the air,
Blue breadths of sea, between wide-spread oak-boughs,
    Life and joy everywhere !

Then royal youth asserts forgotten rights,
    Queen o'er the feeble blood,
Dead hope begins to stir, and visions bright
    The brain's cold chambers flood

Again with warmth and rosy light ; but quick,
    And sharp as kinsmen's strife,
With sudden shock upon the trembling heart,
    Back rolls the tide of life.

And I remember all 'the heavy change,'
    In joy I have no part,
Nor in the glory and the loveliness,
    For death is in my heart.

O rosy light beyond the western hill,
    That fades away so fast !
O life that was so sweet, O joy divine !
    Why are ye of the past ?

And still the lark trills high ; from these fair things
    Their joy will not depart,
Life, life on land and sea, in the fine air,
    Death only in my heart !

TO MADAME D——.

On receiving a letter from Russia describing the cold and deep snow of
April.

I would you heard, as I hear now,
   The song of birds about the eaves,
I would you saw, as I see now,
   The wonder of the new-born leaves.

I would you felt the soft sea breeze
   Blow, as it blows upon my brow,
The rooks are cawing from the trees,
   There is much mirth and music now.

You cannot hear—you will not see
The sweetness of the little isle,
But though you never come to me,
To you I travel many a mile ;

' The narrow seas' I cross again,
I wander over many lands,
Not knowing travel-soil or pain,
Not needing help from any hands.

And when I gain the northern snows,
I see the great pine forest bend
Before the icy blast that blows,
I hear the hungry cries that rend

The frosty air—the flying feet
Of wolves I hear, now loud, now low,
I pass unharmed—my steps more fleet,
That leave no footprint on the snow.

I reach your town, I enter there,
  A silent guest whom no one greets,
I hardly feel the piercing air,
  I pass so quickly through the streets ;

Until I see the house I know
  Heedless am I of bolt or bar,
With warmth and light the windows glow,—
  I find the chamber where you are ;

Glide in, and none my name will call,
  As noiseless I sink down to rest,
While on the hearth the embers fall,
  I lay my head upon your breast,

And murmur a strange word and sweet,
  Do you not feel the shadowy kiss,
A sense as though you ought to greet
  Someone you think you see, yet miss ?

I hear the talk, or grave, or gay,
  I join in laughter or in sighs,
And then a mute ' farewell ' I say,
  For now my spirit homeward flies.

I lift my dreaming eyes—I lie
  Upon the island's yellow shore,
The grey sea merged in greyer sky.
  The long waves breaking evermore.

But here are eyes of such dear worth,
  Hearts beating near, so kind and true,
Would fain make me forget the north,
  And my far travelling to you ;

It may not be—for never more
  Can I forget that which has been,
But these grow dearer than of yore,
  For all that I have felt and seen.

TOO LATE.

We have beheld the stern sad face
    That men call Fate ;
And we have known the kind and fair,
    That comes too late.

Have we not seen the sunny sky
    After the rain ?
But the pale lily by the storm laid low
    Rise not again ?

The dear light sudden shining from the shore,
    For them that roam,
Too late—the good ship strike and sink,
    In sight of home.

The perfect work, after long years of pain,
 The expectant glow—
The great heart broken, waiting for the praise
 That came, too slow.

The cup of costly wine pressed to pale lips,
 Fainting for lack,
Too late—an eager hand stretched quick to take,
 In death fall back.

The little word of truth so long delayed,
 Spoken at last,
But with no power to heal the cruel wound,
 Poisoning the past.

The long night cease—dawn break—but on closed eyes.
 Too tired to wait—
The love that could have saved from worse than death,
 Come, but too late

SAN GIUSEPPE.

Jesuit convent hospital at Naples.

In the darkened chambers there,
  Where Italy's sons are lying,—
Many how young and fair,
  Among the doomed and the dying !

Gently the warrior bends
  O'er each couch where a comrade lies,
His countenance is as the Christ's,
  Like the Saviour's his sorrowful eyes.

Tenderly touching the forehead,
 Tenderly taking the hand
Of a young Venetian, bleeding
 To death for his native land,

Whispered, 'My son, is there aught
 I can do for thee?' Gasping for breath,
The boy murmured, 'Never forget
 My country,'—then sobbed to death.

Pale grew the cheek of the Hero,
 Pale as the face that was dead ;
' If I forget thy country,
 May God forget me,' he said.

1860.

'MORIENS CANO.'

The picture of the Christian martyr.

I hear the shouts that ring,
The hoarse and sullen cry—
The tumult rises high,
The people madly fling
Cruel, clenched hands out to me :
    Dying I sing,
    Glory to thee.
This triumphant jubilee,
Is it theirs or mine ?
Is this, in fine,
Life taken, or life given,
This hurrying me to heaven ?

Forgive them, Christ, they know not what they do !
For well Thou knowest, few
Have learned to tread the narrow way.
That leads through labour to the light of day.
While fierce faces round me glare,
    While cruel voices ring,
Where is the victory ? where ?
    Dying I sing.
Dark and swift the river flows,
In deepening red the sunset glows,
Soon I too shall win repose,
And this weary weight of woes,
Slipping clean from heart and brain,
    Leave me free !
Then for the endless gain !
    Finished the strife,
Ended the agony
    Of death in life ;
All yearning over now,
There, crowns for many a brow,

Full meek and lowly here.
Love only now, no fear—
    Dying I sing.
No more, dear earth, I cling
To thy fair breast, but deep,
Deep now I dare to sleep ;
Never more
To waken, till I touch the blessed shore.
The echoes die away,
    The cruel echoes die,
Fades the last light of day,
    In yonder blood-red sky.
I see the faces bright
Of saints in glory !
Angels bring
To me my raiment, all wash'd white
In blood of Him who died to save.
Where is thy sting,
O death ? Thou watery grave,

Where is thy victory ?
  Dying I sing.
O God ! the tender Father,
Dear Christ, the elder Brother !
The strong holy Comforter !
And Mary, sweet sad mother.
  Dying I sing !

TO MADAME D——.

A little song I thought to send
  On this your natal day,
But though my heart is very full
  Few words I find to say.

The streamlet, breaking from the hills,
  Babbles to rock and tree,
But grown a river deep and wide,
  Flows soundless to the sea.

The birds in summer cease the song
  They warbled in the spring,
For silence seemeth best to them
  That have too much to sing.

For who can tell his joy's excess,
   Or set a tune to sorrow ?
Nor shall I sing in words your worth,
   But of their wisdom borrow !

FOR THE LAST TIME.

'C'était une douce habitude,
Celle de vous voir tous les jours.
Hélas! chaque chose a son cours.
Tout fuit' . . . .

For the last time, rejoicing in the sunlight,
On thy fair waters, Léman, flashing bright ;
The tender shadows on thy mountain wall,
And from thy woods the crimson showers that fall.
For the last time !

For the last time to pass together,
In the golden autumn weather,
By the pathway that we know,
Where listening walnut-trees bend low,
For the last time !

For the last time, beneath the mulberries
(There, where 'the muse of Moscow' rests at ease,
Forgetting the world's noise, and fever heat),
To hear the wise discourse, and laughter sweet,
   For the last time !

For the last time to watch the glowing west,
And the pallor on the mountains, as if prest
The life-blood on a heart that, almost broken,
Waits motionless a word that must be spoken,
   For the last time !

For the last time to see the moonlight stealing
Over vine and cedar, and revealing
The ancient roof that has grown dear,
Till every gable shineth clear,
   For the last time !

For the last time—words of too sad a tone.
And not for us, but for great death alone !
Listen, my heart—who can foretell, or see,
While life is ours, what may, or may not be,
For the last time ?

'NUNC DIMITTIS.'

Lay me beneath the grass,
    Where it slopes to the south and the sea,
Where the living I love may pass,
    And passing, may think of me.

Lay me beneath the grass,
    Not prisoned in churchyard bed,
Where the living I love may pass,
    Not with the mouldering dead.

Lay me beneath the grass,
    With a cross of wood above,
Where the darling feet may pass,
    The little feet that I love.

You will not lay a weight
  Of stone at my head or feet,
What need of name or date ?—
  You will remember, sweet !

Shed not a single tear
  On the clover above my breast,
I am weary, weary, dear,
  You know I have longed for rest.

But ah ! how shall I go,
  When the hour that comes draws near ?
I, who have loved you so,
  How part with all that is dear ?

Lay me beneath the grass,
  When the sweet south wind shall blow,
They will often often pass,
  The footsteps that I know.

'Tis an ancient song, and tender,
　　There be some who know it not,
By many 'tis learned too lightly,
　　By many too soon forgot.

'Tis a melody rare and sweet,
　　With a burden wild and strong,
Sadder than sound of breaking waves,
　　The echoes lingering long.

Clearer and softer than moonlight,
　　Subtle and swift as air,
No singing of birds in woodland
　　May with that song compare.

A flood of mysterious music,
    That makes the low earth divine ;
They know the large hope of immortals,
    Who breathe its enchantment fine.

For the angels lean and listen
    From the dark and silent sky,
The passionate stars to hear it
    Grow mad, and fall from on high !

O bonny bonny hang the trees !
   But and the hedges braw,
The 'tane wi' scarlet and wi' gowd,
   The 'tither wi' hip and haw.

And wan wan is yon wild water,
   Wan now is the burn sae fair,
The bracken is brown on the bonny hillside,
   And, oh ! but my heart is sair.

I'm weary o' the dule and pain
   O' this warld's wae and sin,
And fain fain wad I rest wi' thee,
   Gin ye wad let me in.

Ye sleep sae still, ye sleep sae sound,
   Beneath the birken tree—
It's little ye reck o' the wind and rain.
   And little ye care for me !

POLAND.

'Post tenebras lux.'

I.

Low lies thy head,
O thou forsaken, grieved in spirit, and not comforted,
  Thou captive, bound by cruel foes,
  Beautiful amid thy woes,
  Dreaming in thy dungeon drear,
  Thy love, and thy deliverer near,
  To heal all wounds, and calm all fear,
But waking, find him not, nor arm, nor voice to cheer.
  Trust not in princes, or the word of kings,
  But in the power that brings
  To light all hidden things.

Trust not in princes, or the lofty ones,
　　Who for themselves, and not for thee, will scheme,
But lean upon the love of thine own sons,
　　Who bleed for thee, and dream
But of thy destiny ;
They die, that thou may'st see
The divine light of liberty !

II.

Listen how drearily,
From the bare branches of the stately tree,
　　The last leaf rustles down,
　　Wrinkled and brown ;
　　Fair flowers are faded from the earth,
　　Like souls that were too tender, and too pure,
　　That they might well endure
Her poverty of faith and love, the folly of her mirth.
　　And the fierce northern blast has swept
　　Over the rivulet that leapt

In joy adown the hill,
Where all is now so still,—
And changed it into stone.
It hangeth there alone,
In icy chains fast bound,
Making no sound,
And the whole land is shrouded silently,
In cerements white beneath a frozen sky.
But see, look near !
Where folded fast appear
The darlings of the year ;
The tender buds, pressed close and warm,
Hidden from the winter's harm.
This is not death, but the deep sleep of spring,
And she shall wake, and bring
Her treasures with her—murmurs of the dove,
Sweet flowers, and babbling brooks, that breathe one
language—love.
There is no death ; from darkness and decay
Springs the young life, and wakes the new-born day.

III.

After the darkness, light !
After the long long night
Of weeping, and lone watching, breaks the morn !
    With balmy breath,
    Scattering in bright scorn
    The black battalions of the night,
The terrors of great darkness, and of death :
    And in their stead,
    He cometh, flashing fire !
    The young Day, the desire
    Of longing eyes,
So weary, waiting for the morning red !
    O passing fair,
    After that long despair,
    The wondrous birth
    Of Dawn, in the soft skies !
The splendour of a new-created earth.

In every solitude,

The babblers of the wood,

Breaking the bonds of silence, and of night,

Renew their ancient right

In ecstasy of song !

To them that suffer long,

At last is given

The light from heaven,

The glory of a day,

That never more shall fade or pass away.

'HOPE IS A BONDSMAN—DESPAIR IS FREE.'

You are a slave, my dear,
  Bound hard with a heavy chain,
Forged of a thousand subtle links
  Of doubt, and fear, and pain.

Free as the wind am I,
  Free as the birds of the air,
My liberty knows no limit,
  My freedom is called despair.

THE PAST.

Ah, if by wishing I could bring it back !
    Or by much weeping make it live anew—
Or if by waiting I should see it here,
    Or by long watching find it once more true !
But I may wish, and weep, and wait, and watch in vain,
For it will never more come back to me again.

THE MYRTLE.

According to the customs of the Sheviri, the lover presented the maiden with a flowering plant, which she put out in the porch of her father's house. If she suffered the flower to wither and die, it signified that she would have nothing to say to the lover's suit.'

Once I had a myrtle,
    Blew within my bower,
A fairer myrtle never
    Put forth whiter flower.

O myrtle rare, dear myrtle,
    How bridal-sweet you shone !
Or in the golden sunlight,
    Or in the moonlight wan.

I looked forth in the morning
From the high balcony,
All of carved oak was wrought
The quaint old gallery ;

Roses hung in garlands there,
Passion-flowers climbed up to me.
Fruitful vines and clematis
Had woven a canopy.

There I set my myrtle,
My myrtle proud and high,
To see the sunny lawns and glades,
The blue of lake and sky.

And I forgot the bitter ' bise,'
That sweeps from distant peaks of snow,
From many a glacier icy-cold,
And where the crimson snow-flowers blow.

I only saw the cloudless sky,
  The mountains resting calm and clear,
I only saw the bluer lake,
  And thought that all was sunny here.

I left my myrtle bright as morn,
  With glossy leaves, and fragrant bloom,
When I came back the sun was set,
  The darkening gallery was a tomb,

That held my myrtle, once so fair;
  But life and beauty now were fled,
Shrivelled the blossom, shrunk the leaves—
  My myrtle dear was dead !

And I may water it with tears,
  Shelter it close within my bower,
Nor ever more see glossy leaves,
  Nor ever more the sweetest flower !

' But many myrtles bloom and fade,'
　You say—' and slight should be my pain,'
Yet I would give—what would I not ?—
　To see that myrtle blow again !

QUITS.

'L'avais-je même jamais aimée? Je l'ignore. Je sais seulement, que lorsqu'on n'aime plus, on ne se souvient guère d'avoir aimé.'

Now we are quits, my dear,
   We are equals, I and you.
And I can forget the old days,
   If you can forgive the new.

Did I indeed love you once?
   In truth, when I try to recall,
Not a trace remains, not an echo wakes—
   Like you, I forget it all!

As the dawn dispels the darkness,
   As the day forgets the night,
So the false dream fades for ever,
   In the sunshine of my delight.

Who would have thought it, sweet?
   When I swore to untruth to be true,
That I should break every vow I made,
   And be as forsworn as you?

And yet so it is, my dear,
   Though love cannot die, we know,
Love cannot die, and never was born,
   Immortal, is it not so?

But love is a child, you perceive,
   That only is half divine,
Feed him, and he grows great and strong,
   But he faints for lack of wine!

Quits.

To revive at a tender touch,
   At the smile of a face that is fair,
To look laughing in eyes of light,
   To see himself mirrored there.

But never, believe me, sweet,
   Shall I whisper to you my bliss,
Only to listening stars,
   On a night as fair as this !

'*HEIMWEH.*'

How beautiful she lies, and fair
As any lily—braided hair
   Dark brown on the white brow,
   As cold as marble now !
To the great city she had come—
   Where fades the faultless red
   Of lip and cheek—last night she said,
' I wish I could go home.'

How still she lies—she, who to-day
Thought to have travelled miles away !
Round is the smooth young cheek, but ah, how white !
And white the deep-fringed lids that hide the bright

And tender eyes, too true to roam ;
　　Where is their love-light fled ?
　　Only last night she said,
' I wish I could go home.'

　The words she spake were sweet
　Last night—'Where shall I meet,
　　Far off, in the strange lands,
　　Hearts as true and hands
　　As kind as those at home ?'
　To-day they found her dead—
　Then they remembered the sweet words she said.
　　And knew she had gone home.

'TOUT LASSE, TOUT PASSE, TOUT CASSE!'

If I had been more great.
  Or you had had more skill,
We might have kept our state
  In the house upon the hill.

Or had there been no weight
  Of woe, no wound to still—
Then we had kept our state
  In the house upon the hill.

Surely it was too late,
  Or but a wavering will—
Else we had kept our state
  In the house upon the hill.

It cannot be that hate
  Crept in, and strove to fill
The thrones where love held state
  In the house upon the hill?

Vainly reply we wait—
  The hearts are changed and still,
That in summer held high state
  In the house upon the hill,

I know not was it Fate,
  Or frost with power to kill,
But I know we lost our state
  In the house upon the hill.

.

'*NOSTALGIE.*'

'Dahin! dahin!
Möcht' ich mit dir, o mein Geliebter ziehn.'

Had I the wings of a dove,
  Where do you think I would flee?—
'No doubt very far above
  This naughty low world and me!'

Never, oh never, my love,
  What, without thee, were heaven!
If only the wings of a dove
  For an hour to me were given,

K

Over the bitter sea-foam
  Ah ! how fast would I fly
To the land that was once my home,
  You know it as well as I.

The land of the torrent and mountain,
  And the hearts so friendly and true,
Where we lingered by many a fountain
  And lake that was deep and blue.

Fly with me (I fail and perish
  In this region of mist and gloom),
To the scenes our memories cherish—
  For here is no life, but a tomb !

A very fine land it may be
  For the great, or the proud, caring nought
For sunshine and laughter free,
  That can never be sold or bought !

Where letters, and friendship, and love.
May all be enjoyed, it is clear,
And each has its price marked above
Quite plainly, ' Five thousand a year !'

A very good country, may be,
For them (I have always heard so)
With the thousands—for you and for me,
The very worst country I know !

Let us fly, for I left my gay heart
Long ago, on a hillside fair,
From these gloomy shores let us depart.
For I faint till I find it there !

'*LE PUITS D'AMOUR.*'

'Comment accroit-il sa richesse?
C'est en donnant à chaque pas!'

Whence is this fountain that floweth
　For ever so full and free?
Blest be the warm wind that bloweth
　The waves of the fountain to me!

I give, nor weary of giving
　From the fountain; and still the more
I give of the waters living,
　Fuller they flow than before!

I give—as to me it is given,
    And my sorrow is changed to mirth,
For I think in the hills of heaven
    That fountain must have its birth.

FROM THE GERMAN.

The mountains veil their lofty brows
   In deepest shades of night,
In dewy sleep the valleys lie,
   Close-curtained from the light.

On dusty pathways of the world
   The toil and tumult cease,
Wait thou a little longer, and
   To thee there cometh peace.

FROM THE RUSSIAN OF LERMONTOFF.

A white sail shining in the mist,
    A lonely bark in the blue bay !
What has she left in her own land,
    What seeks she now, so far away ?

The sparkling waves, the whistling wind,
    The mast that sways and creaks ;
Alas ! it is not grief she flies,
    Nor is it joy she seeks.

O'er her the golden sunlight streams,
    Her path is azure-bright and free,
Unsatisfied, she longs for storm—
    As if in storm should comfort be !

THE ISLAND.

FROM THE RUSSIAN OF KOMIAKOFF.

Thou glorious isle, thou wondrous isle !
   Beneath the moon, no gem like thee,
Emerald, thou best and brightest,
   In the blue zone of the sea !
Jealous guardian of thy freedom,
   Fierce destroyer of thy foes,
Grey ocean spreading round thee,
   His strong protection throws.
Deeper than plummet soundeth,
   Spacious and vast is he,   .
He wageth war with all the earth,
   And only loveth thee !

The Island.

Humbled, and subdued before thee,
  While his loud waves rave no more,
How fondly he embraces
  Thy white and shining shore !
O Nature's dearest daughter !
  Happy country, blessed land !
Thy ardent sons press forward,
  With active brain and hand !
How flowery are thy meadows,
  How mighty o'er the seas
Spreads thy wide flag in triumph,
  And floats upon the breeze !
How brightly burns in distant lands
The sword that flashes in thy hands !
The crowns of art and science shed
A glory on thy favoured head;
The music of thy mighty song
Rolls through the world in echoes long !
A shining land of gold far-brought,
And lighted with the light of thought.

Yes, thou art happy, thou art rich,
  Luxuriant, free, and great,
The distant nations trembling raise
  Their longing eyes, and wait,
To learn from thee their destiny,
  The new decrees of fate.
    *   *   *   *   *

But in that thou art treacherous,
  Because thou art so proud,
And lovest less God's judgment,
  Than the world's praises loud ;
And that, with sacrilegious hand,
  Thou dost not ev'n refrain
At the base feet of earthly power
  God's holy church to chain.
For these things, sovereign of the seas,
  There quickly comes a day,
When shrine, and gold, and purple, all,
  Fade like a dream away !

The thunder faileth in thy hands,
　The bright sword burns no more,
Quenched is the clear pure light of thought,
　That shone for thee of yore.
And scorning thy almighty flag,
　All fierce and free again,
Pitiless o'er thy fallen head
　Shall sweep the roaring main !
And to another lowly land,
　Of reverent faith and worth,
Shall God entrust the universe,
　The thunder of the earth ;
And to another shall be given
　To understand the voice of heaven !

THE STARS.

FROM THE RUSSIAN OF KOMIAKOFF.

By the stream at midnight wander,
　And lift up thine eyes on high,
Far into the heavenly regions,
　To the dark and silent sky.
Behold, what wonders are revealed,
　Hidden by the light of day,
These bright orbs of night for ever
　Move round earth harmoniously,
In myriads of quenchless fires !
　Gaze intensely, thou shalt see,
Far away, beyond the nearest,
　Thousands in the galaxy.
Gaze again, and thousands, thousands,
　Blind thine awestruck, fearful eye,

All with stars, and lights unnumbered,
 Glitters the ethereal sky !

At the silent hour of midnight,
 Drive deceiving dreams away,
Raise thy soul from earth and darkness,
 To the realms of endless day.
See what wondrous words are given
 To fishermen of Galilee !
In radiant beauty stars of thought
 Move in mysterious harmony.
A book's small compass doth contain
 A vault as boundless as the sky !
Look long and deep—new thoughts arise,
Gaze more intensely, thy soul's eyes
Shall see those stars of thought and fire,
Thousands, and thousands rising higher ;
Lights of such brightness, without number,
As wake the heart from deepest slumber.

TO J——.

I thought I was dead in the fever-dream,
　And that you had laid me low
In the old churchyard on the hillside steep,
　Where we were wont to go.

The hill that looks down on the ancient church,
　Where the knight in armour stands,
As he has stood for hundreds of years,
　Who once was lord of these lands.

But I thought, though I lay so cold and still,
　I knew when the sunlight burst
On the far yellow fields of Kemmel, bright
　As when we saw them first.

That I knew when the glades of ' Arcady '
    Looked beautiful and fair ;
And I saw the storm come sweeping up
    Through the silent summer air.

And I heard the leaves of the beech we loved
    Shiver in sudden dread
Of the awful rolling thunder, and
    The lightning that flashed o'erhead.

And I knew that the pines were sighing, on
    The hill I should see no more,
Like the sound of the long long waves that roll
    And break on the island shore.

And I felt, when the night was very fair,
    That the wasted moonlight shone
Through the ruined arches of Hohenstein,
    On rock, and on water wan.

And among all the faint pale gleaming ones,
　Our 'bright particular star'
Burned on for ever; though never more
　We should watch it from afar.

And I knew I was lying leagues from them
　That were dearer than life to me,
Sleeping away from all that I loved,
　In my own land over the sea.

I thought you were cruel to leave me there,
　On the cold hillside, alone—
For ever alone—so dark and drear,
　Hearing the night-wind moan.

But you came with the morn—and baleful dreams
　Fled with the phantoms of night,
O, joy ! to find I was not alone,
　Shut out from love and light !

A MIDSUMMER DAY'S DREAM.—TO M. T.

' Never, believe me, appear the immortals, never alone.'

I lie beside the vines and ripening figs,
Above my head there bends a bluer sky
Than over thine—and breathes a softer wind
Beneath this ancient lime-tree's liberal shade.
Than stirs among your lavender and roses.
So high my linden stands, the little airs
That blow in June are never wholly still :
But with an eager importunity,
Murmur among his leaves, and sighing low.
Sway his great branches in the afternoon.
There, down below the vines and orchards—lawns
Shadowed with stately walnuts smelling sweet,

The white shore's mimic bays and capes, beyond
Wide water, and the envious mountain wall,
Hiding the 'promised land'—that Italy
I dream of ; her the mountains may conceal,
But what reveal of their own loveliness,
From early morning's mystery of light
To evening's passionate last farewell flush,
And sad death-pallor which must follow it,
You know.
      But now, though you believe yourself
Blest, breathing English air in the beloved
Quaint garden there—Rossetti painted it,
What time the apples tumble on the grass,
And sun-flowers range against the old red walls—
On distant London though you think you look,
Hearing the throbbings of the world's great heart
Sound through your summer silence—you are here !
Beneath my linden, and beside my vines,
And you have talked with me the livelong day

Wisely, as is your wont, but I—'tis mine—
Laughing at this, and scorning that, though oft
Loving that most which most I seem to scorn.
Shakespeare our theme, the festivals and noise
They vex his bones withal—and then you said.
' I too will celebrate our Shakespeare's feast
' With music and rejoicing—fair young girls
' Shall personate his noblest heroines,
· But how to choose of these immortal ones !—
· My living pictures you must help to group.'
  But was it the long talk, or summer heat,
Or murmuring leaves, or the red wine of France—
I know not ; but I could not choose—I slept !

Then, powers of Tragedy and Comedy defend me !
Of Shakespeare's heroines I saw enough—
Ye gods, how they swept past me where I lay !
Some with fierce flashing eyes and regal robes—
Young Arthur's mother, Henry's angry queen,

And Gertrude with her guilty heart in twain ;
The lithe Egyptian, couched on Tyrian silks,
And lifting langorous eyes of liquid fire—
There, wringing her white hands, that never more
Arabian perfumes might wash clean again,
Macbeth's relentless dame.
                              Grand Portia,
Her satellite, and little Jessica,
That night at Belmont, laughing at the rings.
' The lovely lady wedded to the Moor,'
And Viola, who surely ' told her love ! '
Within the tapestried chamber Imogen
Lay sleeping ;—and, beneath the forest trees,
I heard the laughter of sweet Rosalind ;
Saw her, through all disguise of shepherd-boy,
A fallen Princess and a woman still.
Then deeply-wounded Hero's guileless face—
Beside her, with strong arms about her flung
Protecting—worlds of scorn in her bright eyes—

The queen of wit and women—Beatrice,
More chivalrous and wiser than a man !—
My heart rejoiced to look on her.
     Then one,
With steps uncertain, hurried now, now slow,
Flowers in her streaming hair, flowers mixed with
 straw,
A pale changed face, and wide eyes full of woe
Unutterable—at that cry I woke—
' O, Rose of May, sweet sister, dear Ophelia ! '

1864.

A SILVER WEDDING-DAY.

The whole earth doth rejoice
On this fair day of June,
All nature with one voice
Singeth a happy tune ;
The woods are full of glee,
Of a joyous melody,
A hymn of praise,
Wakening dear memories of other days.
The little birds know well
Your silver wedding-day,
The roses too can tell,
Blushing, of happy Junes now far away.

Over the tall ripe grass
No shadows pass,
  All things are laughing
  To-day, and quaffing
The summer sunshine bright,
In the warm June light ;
The Elm is whispering low,
  And to the Cedar tells
  A tale of love, that swells
Into an ecstasy of pure delight.

The yellow Jessamine heaveth
  An odorous sigh,
For the discrown'd Lilac grieveth,
  And the Lilies that lie
Broken-hearted, and dead
Of despair, for the Spring that is fled.

But the Roses' joy
Knoweth not alloy,
And the happy children are calling
In the garden that we love,
On golden hair the sunlight falling
Like a glory from above,
Shouts of laughter
Follow after,
Frolic free,
And mimic revelry.

O silver wedding-day so bright and fair !
How many faces there,
Sweet faces débonnair,
Proclaim the joys, the peace of many years :
Though not unmixed with care,
And grief, and fears !
O well-beloved, revered !
Around ye. stand
A yet unbroken band,

Nor have our hearts been seared
    By that worse woe,
    That here below,
Can wring from human eyes the bitter tears.

    But where is he,
    So dear to me
Long ere these merry laughers saw the light ?
    Whose voice is low,
    Whose tender eyes
    Are full of sympathies
For all things in whom life doth flow.
    Ah ! long ago,
In other gardens we have strayed,
    And with one heart and soul
    Together played,
Clasping, with tiny linkèd hands,
    The giant bole
    Of the old fairy tree.

O where is he?
Alone he wanders now, in other lands—
This golden morning,
Like a bride adorning,
Glowing with kisses of the western breeze,
Is evening dim,
Or starlight unto him,
· By the long wash of Australasian seas.'
But he returneth soon,
And though we miss his voice
On this sweet day of June,
When we rejoice,
He will remember there,
Your silver wedding-day so bright and fair.

June 24, 1860.

AN APOLOGY.

To those bright courts that crown high Helicon,
  And touch the skies,
Whose starry thresholds burn with blinding light,
  I lift mine eyes.

Not boldly, or in mood irreverent,
  But full of dread ;
My frail defence of such rash enterprise
  Ah how best plead !

When first the rosy fingers of the morn
  Set free the light,
Opening the shining portals of the day.
  And scattering night ;

Some little bird, weak herald, and unskilled,
  Cannot refrain
Pouring from his full heart, o'ercharged with love,
  A passionate strain.

The lowliest flower that blows beneath the moon
  Delights to raise,
Of faint sweet incense, or of dewy tears,
  A hymn of praise.

And through deep summer dells the slender strea
  Doth onward flow,
Murmuring to the dark woods and happy hills
  In music low.

And chiefly before thee, Melpomene,
  My spirit bows ;
To thee, o'er whose grave eyes majestic bend
  The lofty brows.

Of all the fountains of mysterious tears
　　Thou hast the key,
And every secret source and hidden deep
　　Is known to thee

Of the close sister-springs of joy and woe ;
　　Thou canst divine
The subtle tragedies of heart and brain—
　　They all are thine.

The untrodden shores, the pathless solitudes,
　　Where, sad and lone,
The soul must wander to the silent flood,—
　　These are thine own.

O queen of sorrow and of melody !
　　Who hast the lyre,
Of power to move and melt the souls of men,—
　　And heart of fire ;

Weak am I, all unskilled, and yet I dare
    To crave thy grace,
That I, thy lowliest worshipper, may see
    Thy divine face !

I cannot offer fitting sacrifice
    Of gifts heaven-born,
Reverence and love before thy feet I lay,
    Thou wilt not scorn !